14 DAY
BEVERLY HILLS PUBLIC LIBRARY
7858
D0478582

THE
FRIENDS
of the
Beverly Hills
Public Library

My j Sound Box

by Jane Belk Moncure
illustrated by Linda Sommers

THE CHILD'S WORLD
MANKATO, MN 56001

Library of Congress Cataloging in Publication Data

Moncure, Jane Belk.
My j sound box.

(Sound box books)
SUMMARY: A little boy fills his sound box with many words beginning with the letter "j".
[1. Alphabet] I. Sommers, Linda. II. Title.
III. Series.
PZ7.M739Myj [E] 78-23178
ISBN 0-89565-049-5 -1991 Edition

My "j" Sound Box

"I will find things that begin with my 'j' sound," he said.

"I will put them into my sound box."

But first, Little j put on

his jeans and jacket.

"I will jump," he said.

He jumped over the box like a jumping jack.

Then he jumped into the box.

"I am a jack-in-the-box!" he said.
He jumped up.

Little  jumped up a hill.

"I will jump like Jack and Jill," he said.

He jumped down the hill. Then he saw a...

 jack-o'-lantern.

Did he put the
jack-o'-lantern into
his box?

He did!

Then Little jumped until he saw...

jack rabbits!
Jumping jack rabbits!

Did he put the jumping jack rabbits into
the box with the jack-o'-lantern?
He did.
Then he jumped until he saw...

jays.

The jays cried, "Jay, jay, jay!"

Little  j put them into the box with the jack-o'-lantern and the jack rabbits.

Now the box was full, so...

Little j found a jeep.

He put the box with the jack rabbits, jays, and jack-o'-lantern into the jeep...

and drove into the jungle.

Just then, Little j saw a jaguar!

The jaguar was about to jump on the jack rabbits!

Little held up the jack-o'-lantern and...

the jaguar jumped away!

Little j caught the jaguar. He took him to

so he could not jump on the jack rabbits.

Just then,

Little J saw

Jumbo,

the jolly elephant.

"Jumbo is too big for my sound box," he said.

Little  found a jet. A jumbo jet! It was big enough for the animals and everything else!

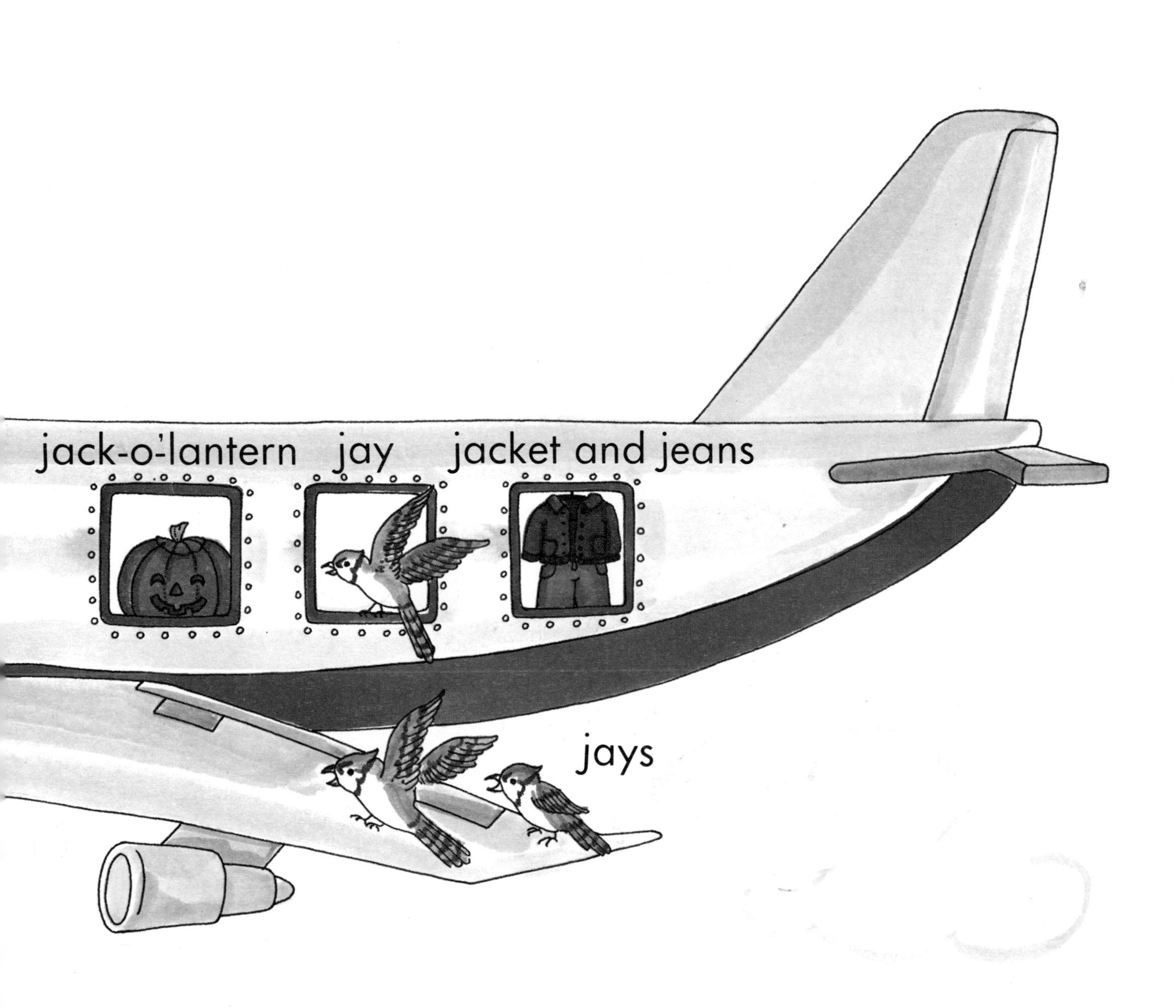
jack-o'-lantern
jay
jacket and jeans
jays

Can you read these words with Little j ?

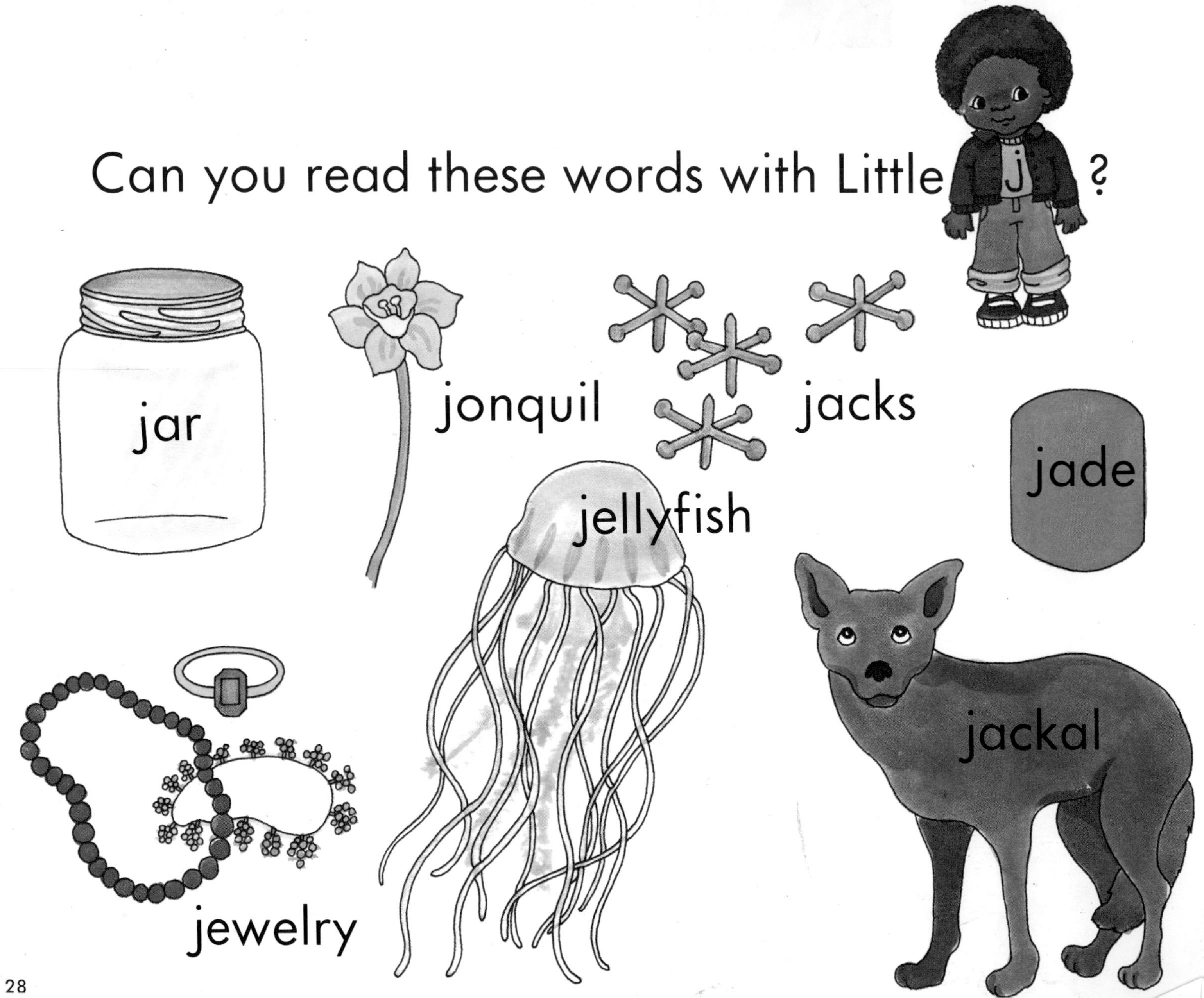

July

s	m	t	w	t	f	s
						1
2	3	4	5	6	7	8
9	10	11	12	13	14	15
16	17	18	19	20	21	22
23/30	24/31	25	26	27	28	29

About the Author

Jane Belk Moncure, author of many books and stories for young children, is a graduate of Virginia Commonwealth University and Columbia University. She has taught nursery, kindergarten and primary children in Europe and America. Mrs. Moncure has taught early childhood education while serving on the faculties of Virginia Commonwealth University and the University of Richmond. She was the first president of the Virginia Association for Early Childhood Education and has been recognized widely for her services to young children. She is married to Dr. James A. Moncure, Vice President of Elon College, and currently teaches in Burlington, North Carolina.